There's a Cow in My Bed
Somos8 Series

© Text: Daniel Fehr, 2022
© Illustrations: Jorge Martín, 2022
© Edition: NubeOcho, 2022
www.nubeocho.com · hello@nubeocho.com

Text Editing: Caroline Dookie, Rebecca Packard

First Edition: March, 2023
ISBN: 978-84-18599-69-9
Legal Deposit: M-13425-2022

Printed in Spain.

THERE'S A COW IN MY BED

Daniel Fehr
Jorge Martín

nubeOCHO

"Why are you still up, dear?"

"I can't go to bed, Dad…"

"There's a cow in my bed!"

"There is no cow in your bed."

"But, but! There was a cow… It's true!"

"Time to go to sleep. Besides, you know? Cows don't like to sleep alone. Why don't you go ask her to make room for you?"

"Dad thinks I'm making it up.
But there really was a cow in my bed!"

"Dad, the cow's back! She's brought her friend, the duck, and they are playing cards. The cow is losing and looks quite grumpy. With a grumpy cow in my room, I surely can't go to bed!"

"Where is the cow and her friend?"

"Maybe they're playing hide-and-seek now. It's no fun to play cards with a grumpy cow all night long."

"Then you can go to bed."

"Dad!"

"What now? I thought they were all gone and your bed was empty."

"The cow and the duck are gone, but now there's an elephant sitting on my bed counting backwards."

"Dear, there is no cow, no duck and no elephant here. Look, your bed is completely empty! Now, it's time to go to sleep!"

"There *was* a cow in my bed, I'm sure of it…"

"Good night."

"Good night, Dad."

"Such a wild imagination my little one has!
Time to go to bed, finally."

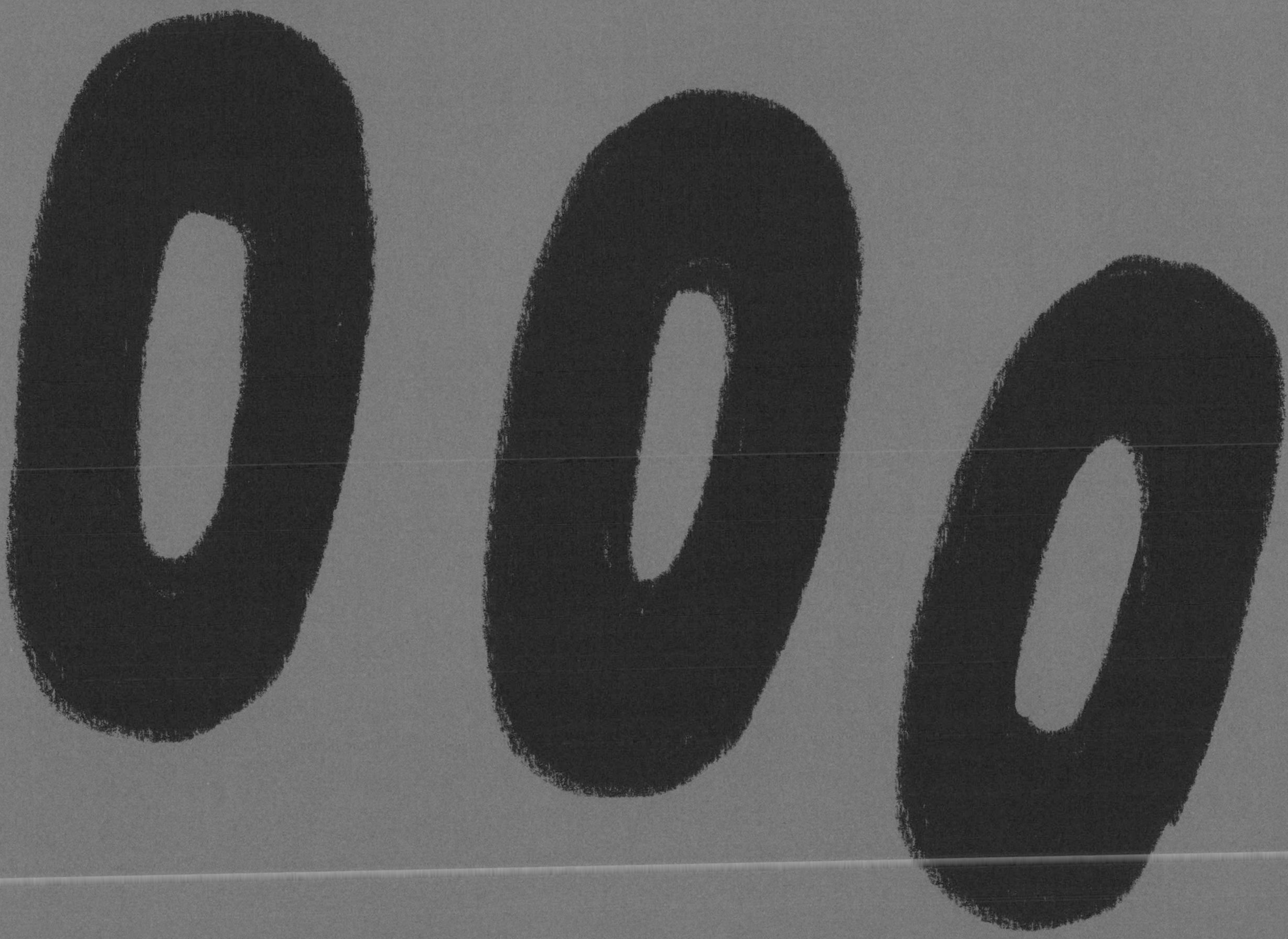

"Dad?!"

"Dear? There's…
There's…"

"There's a cow in my bed!"